For Stella
L.C.

This compilation copyright © 1989 by Laura Cecil
"The Voracious Vacuum Cleaner" copyright © 1989 by Laura Cecil
Illustrations copyright © 1989 by Emma Chichester Clark
First published in Great Britain in 1989 by The Bodley Head Ltd.
First published in the United States in 1989 by Greenwillow Books

Printed in Great Britain
First Edition   10 9 8 7 6 5 4 3 2 1

Library of Congress Cataloging-in-Publication Data
Stuff and nonsense / compiled by Laura Cecil;
illustrations by Emma Chichester Clark.
p.   cm.
Summary: Stories, poems, and traditional tales in which
inanimate things come to life. All are suitable for reading aloud.
ISBN 0-688-08898-8   1. Children's literature.
[1. Literature—Collections.]   I. Cecil, Laura.
II. Clark, Emma Chichester, ill.   PZ5.S898   1989
808.8′99282—dc19   89-1647   CIP   AC

STUFF
AND
NONSENSE

Compiled by Laura Cecil
Illustrated by
Emma Chichester Clark

Greenwillow Books
New York

ACKNOWLEDGEMENTS

Thanks are due to the following for permission to reprint copyright material: Peter Dixon for 'I'd Like to Be a Teabag' from *Grow Your Own Poems*. Copyright © 1988 Peter Dixon. Published by Macmillan Education Ltd. 'The Shepherdess and the Chimney Sweep' by Hans Andersen. This translation © 1989 Naomi Lewis. Reprinted by permission of Naomi Lewis. 'The Macaronies Who Went for a Walk' by Milos Macourek from *Pohadky*. Published by ARTIA. Reprinted by permission of Milos Macourek. English translation from Czech © 1980 Marie Burg from *Curious Tales*. Published by Oxford University Press 1980. William Jay Smith for 'The Toaster' from *Laughing Time: Nonsense Poems*. Copyright © 1955, 1957, 1980 by William Jay Smith. Published by Delacorte Press. Reprinted by permission of William Jay Smith. 'My TV Came Down with a Chill!' from *A Children's Almanac of Words at Play*. Copyright © 1982 by Willard R. Espy. Reprinted by permission of Clarkson N. Potter, Inc. and Hodder & Stoughton Limited. J. M. Dent & Sons Limited for 'The Pumpkins of Witch Crunch' by Margaret Mahy from *The Great Chewing Gum Rescue*. Copyright © 1982 Margaret Mahy. 'The Lonely Skyscraper' by Jenny Hawkesworth. Copyright © 1980 Jenny Hawkesworth. First published by Methuen Children's Books in association with Walker Books Limited. Reprinted by permission of Walker Books Limited. 'Forty Performing Bananas' from *The New Kid on the Block* by Jack Prelutsky. Text copyright © 1984 by Jack Prelutsky. Reprinted by permission of Greenwillow Books (A Division of William Morrow and Company Inc.). 'Brown Paper' from *The Little Knife who did all the Work* by Alison Uttley. Copyright © 1962 Alison Uttley. Reprinted by permission of Faber and Faber Ltd. 'Don't Blame Me!' from *The Wonder Dog* by Richard Hughes. Copyright © 1940 Richard Hughes. Published by Chatto & Windus and Greenwillow Books (A Division of William Morrow and Company Inc.). Reprinted by permission of David Higham Associates Limited, London.

Traditional Sources: 'The Sorcerer's Apprentice' from *Der Zauberlehring* by Goethe. This retelling © 1989 Laura Cecil. 'The Magic Tea-kettle' from 'The Magic Kettle', *Crimson Fairy Book* ed. Lang 1909; 'The Good Fortune Kettle' by Haviland from *Favourite Fairy Tales Told in Japan* 1967; 'The Dancing Kettle' by Uchida from *The Dancing Kettle and Other Japanese Folktales* 1949. This retelling © 1989 Laura Cecil.

Laura Cecil would like to give special thanks to Adèle Geras for her help in finding some original source material and generously making available her collection of *Cricket* magazine.

Introduction

My father loved reading aloud. When I was a small child I would wander into his study and, if he was not busy, he would read to me for a few minutes before going on with his work. He liked to read fairy tales, particularly Hans Andersen, who was one of his favorite authors. One story I especially enjoyed was 'The Shepherdess and the Chimney Sweep'. I loved the idea that objects in a room had their own lives and dramas, unseen by the people around them. I felt I could look at anything in our house and construct such a world myself.

I think this is the core of what children enjoy about the kind of story in this collection: stories in which "stuff" or inanimate things come alive. Hans Andersen was a master of this form and his fairy tales have done more than any others to make the idea popular. His genius was that when he brought an object to life, he gave it a personality that reflected its essential characteristics. In 'The Shepherdess and the Chimney Sweep', a whole room comes alive: from a grotesque baroque cupboard and a nodding china mandarin, to the fragile porcelain ornaments of the title. I would like to think the story was inspired by a real place, and that Andersen told it to some children to explain why a china mandarin was found mysteriously broken on the floor. Alison Uttley achieves the same fusion of object and character with what at first seems unpromising material: a piece of brown paper. But its modest and dependable personality seems entirely believable. Some objects have such strong personalities that they can inspire a whole story. Jenny Hawkesworth told me that she was waiting for a bus one evening, when she suddenly noticed how sad and uncared for a skyscraper looked as all the workers streamed out of it. This gave her the idea for 'The Lonely Skyscraper', which tells the story of an office building that longs to be somebody's home.

Folk tales about objects have their origin in the idea that spirits or devils can enter inanimate things. North European folklore has many examples of domestic objects – pans, brooms or food – possessed by fairies or devils. In later versions, the devil or poltergeist element is often left out and the object becomes alive in its own right. The Japanese story 'The Magic Tea-kettle' is unusual in that the spirit in the kettle is a benign one. In this story the spirit helps the kettle's owner to make his fortune, but not at anybody else's expense. The story teaches generosity and civilized behavior. This is in contrast to the vindictive spirits found in many European stories, like 'The Sorcerer's Apprentice' – itself an example of how, in Nordic folklore, witches and warlocks have objects rather than black cats as their familiars. The story of a runaway pancake or gingerbread man is one of the best known folk tales and has many versions. I have chosen 'Johnny-cake' from Joseph Jacobs' fairy tales, which he took from a North American source, as it has vigor and deadpan humor not found in other, better known tellings.

Margaret Mahy uses the folk tale theme of possession in her story 'The Pumpkins of Witch Crunch', where a witch takes revenge by setting some pumpkins on their disagreeable owner with splendidly comic effect. I have borrowed from folklore myself in 'The Voracious Vacuum Cleaner'. The nonsense story where a creature swallows an impossible quantity of people and things, is told all over the world: the main character ranging from a cat in India, to a giant wooden baby in Czechoslovakia. Using a vacuum cleaner to make a modern version seemed an obvious choice, as many children wonder at the machine's apparent capacity to swallow anything. I can remember hating the roaring noise and being half afraid that I might disappear along with the dust.

When objects behave like humans, there is an inherent absurdity that lends itself especially to nonsense stories and poems. The art of nonsense humor is to make an impossible situation seem natural and logical. By the end of 'The Macaronies who went for a Walk', Milos Macourek makes the reader accept not only macaronies in mackintoshes going for a walk, but also cooked and raw macaronies carrying on a conversation in a restaurant – some on a plate and the others sitting round the table! Lear's table and chair argue with each other about whether they can walk, and the table suggests with impeccable nonsense logic:

'It can do no harm to try,
I've as many legs as you,
Why can't we walk on two?'

The wealth of modern inventions is a gift to nonsense writers and poets: televisions, toasters and tea-bags all feature in this collection. Modern methods of transport have been the inspiration for many of the most popular stories where an inanimate object has a life of its own. Apart from Richard Hughes' bewitched motorbike in 'Don't Blame Me!', I have not included any of these because the best are picture books, where the text is inseparable from the original illustrations. It is impossible to imagine *Mike Mulligan and his Steam Shovel* without Virginia Lee Burton's own pictures or Graham Greene's *The Little Train* without Ardizzone.

I cannot imagine making a collection like this without Emma Chichester Clark's illustrations, as we share the same liking for fantastic stories and surrealist humor. In our first collaboration, *Listen to This*, I was delighted by her skill in capturing the spirit of the stories I had chosen, so I have particularly enjoyed finding material which I thought would appeal to her special imagination.

Laura Cecil

Contents

Johnny-cake

JOSEPH JACOBS

Once upon a time there was an old man, and an old woman, and a little boy. One morning the old woman made a Johnny-cake, and put it in the oven to bake. "You watch the Johnny-cake while your father and I go out to work in the garden." So the old man and the old woman went out and began to hoe potatoes, and left the little boy to tend the oven. But he didn't watch it all the time, and all of a sudden he heard a noise, and he looked up and the oven door popped open, and out of the oven jumped Johnny-cake, and went rolling along end over end, towards the open door of the house. The little boy ran to shut the door, but Johnny-cake was too quick for him and rolled through the door, down the steps, and out into the road long before the little boy could catch him. The little boy ran after him as fast as he could clip it, crying out to his father and mother, who heard the uproar, and threw down their hoes and gave chase too. But Johnny-cake outran all three a long way, and was soon out of sight, while they had to sit down, all out of breath, on a bank to rest.

On went Johnny-cake, and by and by he came to two well-diggers who looked up from their work and called out: "Where ye going, Johnny-cake?"

He said: "I've outrun an old man, and an old woman, and a little boy, and I can outrun you, too-o-o!"

"Ye can, can ye? We'll see about that!" said they; and they threw down their picks and ran after him, but couldn't catch up with him, and soon they had to sit down by the roadside to rest.

On ran Johnny-cake, and by and by he came to two ditch-diggers who were digging a ditch. "Where ye going, Johnny-cake?" said they.

He said: "I've outrun an old man, and an old woman, and a little boy, and two well-diggers, and I can outrun you, too-o-o!"

"Ye can, can ye? We'll see about that!" said they; and they threw down their spades, and ran after him, too. But Johnny-cake soon outstripped them also, and seeing they could never catch him, they gave up the chase and sat down to rest.

On went Johnny-cake, and by and by he came to a bear. The bear said: "Where are ye going, Johnny-cake?"

He said: "I've outrun an old man, and an old woman, and a little boy, and two well-diggers, and two ditch-diggers, and I can outrun you, too-o-o!"

"Ye can, can ye?" growled the bear. "We'll see about that!" and trotted as fast as his legs could carry him after Johnny-cake, who never stopped to look behind him. Before long the bear was left so far behind that he saw he might as well give up the hunt first as last, so he stretched himself out by the roadside to rest.

On went Johnny-cake, and by and by he came to a wolf. The wolf said: "Where ye going, Johnny-cake?"

He said: "I've outrun an old man, and an old woman, and a little boy, and two well-diggers, and two ditch-diggers, and a bear, and I can outrun you, too-o-o!"

"Ye can, can ye?" snarled the wolf. "We'll see about that!" And he set into a gallop after Johnny-cake, who went on and on so fast that the wolf, too, saw there was no hope of overtaking him, and he, too, lay down to rest.

On went Johnny-cake, and by and by he came to a fox that lay quietly in a corner of the fence. The fox called out in a sharp voice, but without getting up: "Where ye going, Johnny-cake?"

He said: "I've outrun an old man, and an old woman, and a little boy, and two well-diggers, and two ditch-diggers, a bear, and a wolf, and I can outrun you, too-o-o!"

The fox said: "I can't quite hear you, Johnny-cake; won't you

come a little closer?" turning his head a little to one side.

Johnny-cake stopped his race for the first time, and went a little closer, and called out in a very loud voice: "*I've outrun an old man, and an old woman, and a little boy, and two well-diggers, and two ditch-diggers, and a bear, and a wolf, and I can outrun you, too-o-o!*"

"Can't quite hear you; won't you come a *little* closer?" said the fox in a feeble voice, as he stretched out his neck towards Johnny-cake, and put one paw behind his ear.

Johnny-cake came up close, and leaning towards the fox screamed out: "I'VE OUTRUN AN OLD MAN, AND AN OLD WOMAN, AND A LITTLE BOY, AND TWO WELL-DIGGERS, AND TWO DITCH-DIGGERS, AND A BEAR, AND A WOLF, AND I CAN OUTRUN YOU, TOO-O-O!"

"You can, can you?" yelped the fox, and he snapped up the Johnny-cake in his sharp teeth in the twinkling of an eye.

I'd Like to Be a Teabag

PETER DIXON

I'd like to be a teabag,
And stay at home all day—
And talk to other teabags
In a teabag sort of way . . .

I'd love to be a teabag,
And lie in a little box—
And never have to wash my face
Or change my dirty socks . . .

I'd like to be a teabag,
An Earl Grey one perhaps,
And doze all day and lie around
With Earl Grey kind of chaps.

I wouldn't have to do a thing,
No homework, jobs or chores—
Comfy in my caddy
Of teabags and their snores.

I wouldn't have to do exams,
I needn't tidy rooms,
Or sweep the floor or feed the cat
Or wash up all the spoons.

I wouldn't have to do a thing,
A life of bliss—you see . . .
Except that once in all my life

I'd make a cup of tea!

The Shepherdess
and the Chimney Sweep

HANS ANDERSEN
Translated by Naomi Lewis

I wonder—have you ever seen a really old wooden cabinet, so old that the wood is quite black, and carved all over with twirling stems and leaves? In the room where this story happened there was a cupboard or cabinet just like that. Once it had belonged to the children's great-great-great-great-grandmother. From top to bottom, every inch of it was covered with carvings; some were of flowers, roses and tulips, with curly lines around, while through the spaces, little wooden deer poked out their antlered heads.

But in the middle was the strangest carving of all—the figure of a man, if you could call him a man. He had legs like a goat's, two small horns coming out of his forehead, a long beard, and a peculiar grin on his face; a grin, not a smile. The children called him BrigadierGeneralFieldMarshalMajorSergeantCorporal-

Goatlegs. It suited him well, that name; for one thing, it was hard to say—and who else could ever reach that rank?

Anyhow, there he was, and all the time his eyes were fixed on the table under the mirror—that was where a little china shepherdess had her special place. She had golden shoes, a golden hat, and a shepherdess's crook in her hand. Her dress was prettily pinned with a china rose. Oh, she was lovely! Just beside her was a little china chimney sweep. His clothes were black as coal, but they were as neat and clean as anyone else's; his face, indeed, was as pink and white as a girl's. Really, he was only a make-believe sweep. The china maker could just as easily have dressed him up as a prince. He looked extremely smart with his ladder and brush and his pretty face which hadn't even a smudge of soot on it. That was wrong, of course. He had been placed by the side of the little shepherdess and because they were always together they became engaged. After all, they were a well-matched pair. Both were young, both were made of the same china clay, and—being so fine—both were equally breakable.

Quite near to them was another character, one about three times their size. This was an old Chinese mandarin. He could nod his head; nod nod, yes yes. He too was made of china, and always claimed (though he couldn't prove it) that he was the young shepherdess's grandfather, guardian and next of kin. So, when BrigadierGeneralFieldMarshalMajorSergeantCorporal-Goatlegs decided to marry the little shepherdess, he went to the old mandarin to ask for his consent. Nod nod went the

17

mandarin, which meant Yes yes, you may.

"You'll have a fine husband," said the mandarin. "I do believe he is made of mahogany—I'm almost certain of it. You will be Mrs Madam Lady BrigadierGeneralFieldMarshalMajorSergeantCorporalGoatlegs. Think of that! He is rich; his cupboard is full of silver dishes—and he has other, secret hoards hidden away, so they tell me."

"I won't go into that dark cupboard," said the little shepherdess. "They say he has eleven wives in there already."

"Then you will be the twelfth," said the old mandarin. "Tonight, just as soon as the cupboard starts creaking, the marriage will take place, I promise you." With that, he nodded his head, nod nod, yes yes, and fell asleep.

The little shepherdess began to cry. She looked up at her china sweetheart and said, "I think I must ask you something. Will you take me out into the wide world? I cannot stay here."

"Whatever you wish, I shall do," said the little chimney sweep. "Indeed we can start at once. I am sure that I can earn enough to support you by my profession."

"Oh, how I long to get down from this table," said the little shepherdess. "I cannot feel safe until we are out in the wide world."

The chimney sweep did his best to comfort her, then carefully showed her where to place one little foot, then the next, on the carved leaves and ledges round the table-leg. He used his ladder too, and at last they reached the ground. But when they looked up at the cupboard, what a to-do! All the carved deer were poking out their heads as far as they could, pricking up their antlers, twisting their necks, now to the left, now to the right. As for Brigadier-

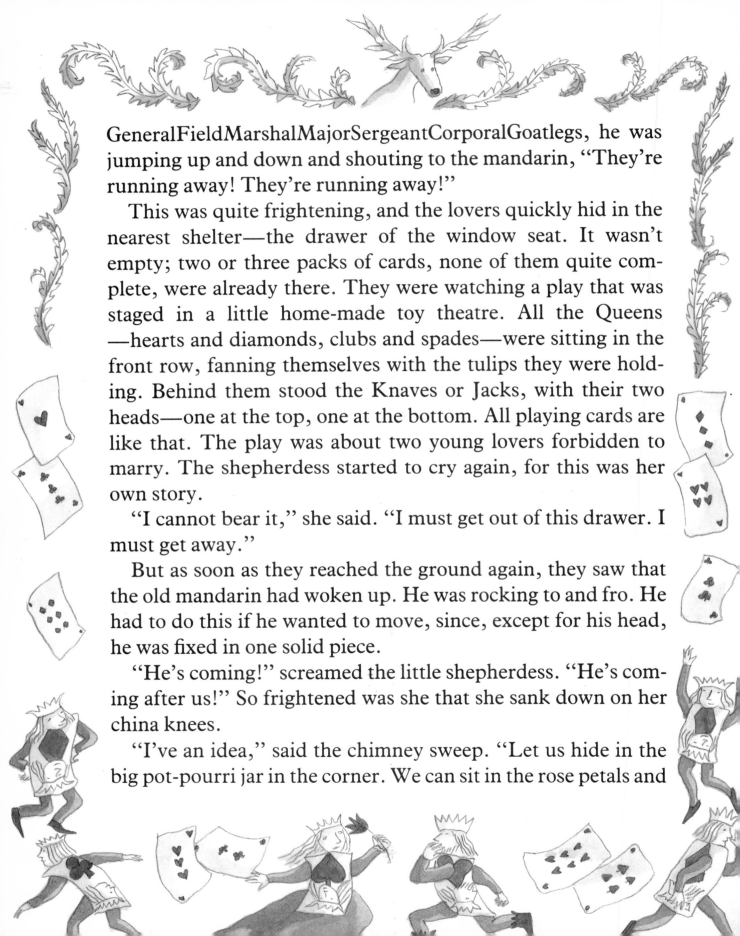

GeneralFieldMarshalMajorSergeantCorporalGoatlegs, he was jumping up and down and shouting to the mandarin, "They're running away! They're running away!"

This was quite frightening, and the lovers quickly hid in the nearest shelter—the drawer of the window seat. It wasn't empty; two or three packs of cards, none of them quite complete, were already there. They were watching a play that was staged in a little home-made toy theatre. All the Queens —hearts and diamonds, clubs and spades—were sitting in the front row, fanning themselves with the tulips they were holding. Behind them stood the Knaves or Jacks, with their two heads—one at the top, one at the bottom. All playing cards are like that. The play was about two young lovers forbidden to marry. The shepherdess started to cry again, for this was her own story.

"I cannot bear it," she said. "I must get out of this drawer. I must get away."

But as soon as they reached the ground again, they saw that the old mandarin had woken up. He was rocking to and fro. He had to do this if he wanted to move, since, except for his head, he was fixed in one solid piece.

"He's coming!" screamed the little shepherdess. "He's coming after us!" So frightened was she that she sank down on her china knees.

"I've an idea," said the chimney sweep. "Let us hide in the big pot-pourri jar in the corner. We can sit in the rose petals and

lavender, and if he comes we can throw salt in his eyes."

"That won't do at all," she said. "Besides, I happen to know that the old mandarin and the pot-pourri jar were once engaged. When people have been as close as that, there is always a friendly feeling left. No, we have no choice but to go out into the wide world."

"Are you really brave enough to come with me into the wide world?" asked the sweep. "Do you know how vast it is? Have you thought that we may never get back again?"

"Yes," she said. "I have thought of that. I do wish to go."

The sweep looked at her keenly. Then he said, "The only way I know lies through the chimney. Think once more. Are you really brave enough to follow me through the heart of the stove and the dark flue tunnel behind? After that comes the chimney itself—a long climb, but easier to manage. We shall climb so high that no one can ever catch us. And when we are at the top there's a round hole that takes us right out into the wide world."

He led her across to the stove.

"Oh, it does look black," she said. But she went with him all the same, through the heart of the stove and the dark flue tunnel behind, where all was as black as night.

"We've reached the chimney now," he said. "Look! There's a lovely star just overhead."

Yes, there was indeed a real bright star, shining down upon them, as if it wished to show the way. On and on they crawled

and crept, up and up, higher and higher—it was a dreadful journey. All the time the sweep kept patiently helping the little shepherdess, showing her the best place for each step of her china feet—until at last they reached the top of the chimney and sat down to rest on the edge of the chimney pot. They were quite worn out, and can you wonder!

They looked around. High above was the sky with all its stars. Down below lay the town with all its roofs. All around was the wide world, stretching far into the distance. The poor little shepherdess had never imagined anything so bewildering. She laid her head on the sweep's shoulder and cried and cried until all the gilt was washed from her sash.

"It is too much!" she cried. "I can't bear it. The world is too big for me. Oh, if only I could be back again in my old place on the table under the mirror! I shall never be happy again until I am there. I came with you into the wide world. Now if you really love me, please take me home."

The sweep spoke to her gently, reminding her of the old mandarin and BrigadierGeneralFieldMarshalMajorSergeant-

CorporalGoatlegs, and all the various dangers they had left. But she did not listen. All she did was weep and weep and cling to her chimney sweep, until at last—though he knew it was foolish—he had to give in to her. What else could he do?

So they began their long hard journey back. They crawled down the chimney, crept through the dark flue tunnel and into the murky cavern of the stove. For a while they stood behind the stove's iron door to hear what was going on. The room seemed oddly quiet, so, presently, they peeped out. But what a shock! There in the middle of the floor, lay the old mandarin. Trying to chase the lovers, he had shaken himself right off the table and now lay on the floor, cracked into three pieces. His back and front had come apart and his head had rolled into a corner. And the BrigadierGeneralFieldMarshalMajorSergeant-CorporalGoatlegs? There he stood, fixed in his usual place, he seemed to be deep in thought.

"This is dreadful!" cried the little shepherdess. "Old grand-father is broken to bits—and it is all our fault. I shall never get over it, never." And she wrung her tiny hands.

"Don't worry, he can still be mended," said the sweep. "That's no problem. Don't get so excited. When they have glued his front and back together and put a rivet in his neck, he'll be as good as new. He'll have plenty of nasty things to say to us yet."

"Do you really think so?" said the shepherdess. Then they climbed back to their old places on the table top.

"Well, here we are, just where we started from," said the

sweep. "We might have saved ourselves all that trouble."

"I do wish old grandfather were mended," said the shepherdess. "Will it be very expensive, do you think?"

The old mandarin was mended. The family had him glued together, and a rivet was put in his neck to join his head to the rest of him. He looked as good as new but there *was* a difference. He couldn't nod any more.

"You *have* become high and mighty since your fall," said BrigadierGeneralFieldMarshalMajorSergeantCorporalGoatlegs. "Though I can't think what you have to be proud about. I want an answer now. Am I to have the shepherdess—yes or no?"

The sweep and the shepherdess watched the old mandarin anxiously. They were afraid that he would nod: yes. But he could no longer do this, and he certainly did not wish to admit that he had a rivet in his neck. So the shepherdess and the chimney sweep stayed together and went on loving each other in perfect happiness, until they broke.

The Sorcerer's Apprentice
GERMAN

ASorcerer lived in a lonely house on the side of a mountain. He was a formidable old man with a bowed back and thick red spectacles that hid his eyes. Now that he was old, he needed an apprentice to help him, so he found a boy who was sharp-witted and eager to learn. At first the boy, whose name was Felix, enjoyed his work. He was fascinated by the strange herbs he had to collect and by the ancient glass jars filled with bubbling mixtures in his master's room. But soon he longed to be able to work spells himself. Yet whenever he asked the Sorcerer to teach him, he was told that he was too young and that magic was dangerous. He must be

26

patient and wait until he had learned more. Felix did not answer
back, but he thought to himself: "The old fool doesn't want me
to learn in case I get the better of him. I'll watch him carefully
and learn that way."

So, day after day, he watched and listened. At night he would
creep down and study the Sorcerer's books when the old man
was asleep. He was especially interested by the way the Sorcerer
was able to summon up spirits to make the things in his
work-room come alive and help him with his magic. At his
command the glass jars full of bubbling mixtures would rise up

and pour themselves into other vessels, and stop as soon as he spoke another magic word. The Sorcerer's favorite object was an old broomstick that he used to help him carry out tasks he thought too difficult or dangerous for Felix. He spoke his magic commands very fast and it was some time before Felix could understand them and learn the words by heart. He longed to try out what he knew, but he did not dare while the Sorcerer was in the house.

Then one day the Sorcerer announced that he had to go out on urgent business: "We have a very important spell to make tonight. I want you to prepare it while I am out. You must fill the marble tub in the middle of my work-room with fresh water from the stream outside. Make sure it is full by the time I return."

So saying he clambered on to a small dragon and flew away. "At last he's gone!" said Felix. "Now I shall be able to call up spirits too! It will take me all day to fill that tub if I carry the water from the stream myself, so let's see what I can use to help me!"

He looked round the work-room and saw his master's broomstick leaning against the wall. He pointed at it and said the magic words of command:

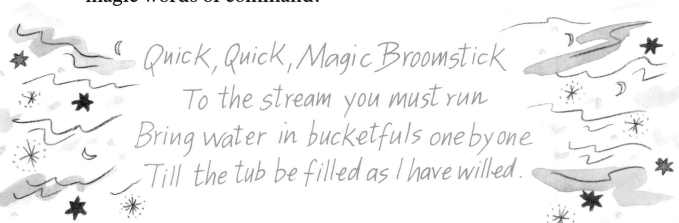

Quick, Quick, Magic Broomstick
To the stream you must run
Bring water in bucketfuls one by one
Till the tub be filled as I have willed.

The broomstick quivered. Its twigs divided into two feet, thin arms sprang out of the handle and a small head grew out of the top. Felix thrust a bucket into its hand and it strode out of the door making a curious rustling sound with its twiggy feet. A moment later it was back from the stream and filling the tub. Back and forth it went, quicker and quicker. "This is better than I could have hoped," thought Felix. "The job will soon be done and I will have lots of time to try out other spells."

He began to study his master's books, but suddenly a slopping noise made him look up. The tub was almost full, but the broom still rustled back and forth emptying the bucket until the tub began to overflow. "Still stand – I mean – stand still O Broom!" cried Felix.

Then he realized to his horror that he could not remember the rest of the spell. Frantically, he searched his master's books for the words. Meanwhile the broom worked quicker and quicker. The tub flooded over on to the floor and soon Felix was ankle-deep in water. But still the broom worked on. It was able to glide on top of the water so that now it made a swishing sound instead of a rustling one.

Felix tried every spell he could remember, but not one had the right words. "Oh how I wish you were an old broomstick again!" he moaned. "There's nothing for it, I'll have to catch you and force you to stop or I shall be drowned."

As the broom swooshed past, Felix grabbed it. The broom turned its head and bit him sharply so that he let go immediately, crying with pain. Its hard wooden eyes glared at him malevolently, but it never slackened its pace. Felix was terrified. What would the Sorcerer say when he came back? Already the water had spread to other rooms, and books and bottles were floating round him higgledy-piggledy.

Then Felix saw an axe hanging on the wall behind him. He seized it and when the broom came by again he aimed a careful blow and split it deftly down the middle. Sighing with relief, Felix flopped down in a puddle of soggy papers. At last the broom had been stopped. Then to his horror he saw the two halves of the broom stand up. Each one now had two twiggy feet, two arms and a malevolent little head on top of the handle. They each seized a bucket and set off for the stream. Now there was twice as much water coming into the house.

Felix tried to snatch the buckets as the brooms strode past but they were too fast for him. Then he seized another bucket and tried to carry some of the water out again, but all to no avail. The brooms only worked faster when they saw what he was trying to do.

Then suddenly he remembered a summoning spell. Desperately, Felix called upon the Sorcerer to appear. There was a clatter of wings and a hiss of steam as the dragon and Sorcerer landed in the water before him. The Sorcerer raised his arms and seemed to grow twice as tall.

Have done O Broom and Broom!
Return to your corner of the room!
Never again shall you live
Until you hear ME orders give!
Flood Begone!
Go back to the stream where you belong.

Instantly the water vanished, the brooms dropped the buckets and hopped into the corner. A second later they fused into one broomstick again which fell with a lifeless clatter against the wall. The Sorcerer picked it up and handed it to Felix. "Now you can use this to sweep up all the mess," he said. "But no more magic."

The Macaronies Who Went for a Walk

MILOS MACOUREK
Translated by Marie Burg

To live in a box and never see a thing—that must be an awful bore. There they were, lying in a box in the larder, bored stiff: about 120 sticks of macaroni. They were Italian macaronies, so they spoke to each other in Italian.

"What a bore," they said, "what a bore."

"It's so boring," said one macaroni, "we're bored to the teeth—in fact, we could end up eating one another."

"Well, we can't eat one another raw," said macaroni number three. "But why don't we go somewhere? The world is so interesting, after all. It has merry-go-rounds and swings and all sorts of concerts, fancy restaurants, zoos, and goodness knows what else."

"All right," said macaroni number nine, "but will they let us go? People will see us and they'll say, 'Ah! Macaronies!' and they'll grab hold of us, and that'll be the end of our walk."

"We mustn't be recognized," said macaroni number thirty-seven, "so let's wear hats and raincoats."

So they put on hats and raincoats and off they went. They walked the streets, all 120 of them, and people said, "Look! Some sort of guided tour."

From time to time the macaronies stopped people who were passing by and asked in Italian, "Excuse us, do you know any interesting sights around here?"

"The trouble is," people said, "we don't know any Italian, but if you want to see something interesting, we've got a merry-go-round and swings, all sorts of concerts, a fancy restaurant, a zoo, and goodness knows what else."

"Well, perhaps we'll try the merry-go-round and the swings first, and then a concert and the zoo," said the macaronies.

"Well, in that case you go such and such a way," people said, and the macaronies walked on and visited the merry-go-round and swings, and a concert, and the zoo.

It was all very interesting, but in the end the macaronies felt cold, their feet were frozen, and they said to one another, "It was all very interesting. All macaronies ought to see things like that. But now let's go and sit down in a restaurant."

So they went into a restaurant, sat down quietly, and chatted together in Italian. When the waiter heard them, he said to himself, "I know how to please them—I'll bring them Italian macaroni. They'll enjoy that!" And that's just what he did—he brought them macaroni.

As you can imagine, it was a pleasant surprise for the macaronies—the ones sitting at the table as well as the ones lying on the plates—and they all said at once, "What a coincidence! What are you doing here?"

"Well," said the macaronies sitting on the chairs, "we were bored stiff, so we went for a little walk and, because our feet were hurting us, we called here."

"Why didn't we think of that before now?" said the macaronies on the plates to one another. "We might have seen something ourselves."

"It's never too late. We've already seen all sorts of things. But you haven't seen any. Let's change places—you take our hats and raincoats, and we'll lie down on the plates. It's quite simple. Let's get on with it!"

So the macaronies that were lying on the plates jumped down on to the carpet. But the head waiter came running up and said to the ones at the table, "Excuse me, I don't know any Italian, but what sort of manners have you got? All the macaroni is on the carpet. I thought you knew how to eat macaroni." And he hurried away to fetch a dustpan and brush.

"Here are the hats and the raincoats," said the first group of macaronies to the second. "Get dressed while we get on to the plates." And they climbed on to the plates, dipped their feet in the hot sauce, and felt fine.

When the head waiter arrived with the dustpan and brush, he saw that there were no macaronies on the carpet and that the guests were leaving. He was very surprised. "Why are you leaving?" he wanted to know. "Didn't you like the macaroni?"

"Excuse us," said the macaronies who were about to leave, "but how could we eat macaroni? Since when is genuine Italian macaroni eaten raw?"

The head waiter looked, and he saw that the macaronies on the plates really were raw. He made his apologies, thinking, "What a disgrace!"

But the macaronies wearing hats and raincoats smiled and said, "Never mind, that can easily happen."

And they waved goodbye to the raw macaronies, and went out to have a look at the swings and the merry-go-rounds and at the whole world that is so very interesting.

The Toaster
WILLIAM JAY SMITH

A silver-scaled Dragon with jaws flaming red
Sits at my elbow and toasts my bread.
I hand him fat slices, and then, one by one,
He hands them back when he sees they are done.

My TV Came Down with a Chill
WILLARD R. ESPY

My TV came down with a chill.
As soon as I saw it was ill
I wrapped up its channels
In warm winter flannels
And gave its antenna a pill.

The Magic Tea-kettle
JAPANESE

High up among the wooded mountains in the middle of Japan lived an old man in a little house. It was a very pretty house and the old man was proud of it. It had white straw mats on the floor and paper walls which could slide open in the warm weather so that the old man could smell the trees and flowers outside.

One day he was looking out at the mountains opposite, when he heard a strange noise in the room behind him. The old man turned round and saw a tea-kettle lying in the corner. He did not know how it could have got there, but he picked it up and looked it over carefully. It was old but undamaged, and he was pleased as he needed a tea-kettle. Smiling to himself, he decided to make some tea. He filled the kettle with water and placed it on a little hibachi stove. But as soon as the water began to get hot an extraordinary thing happened. First the lid of the kettle became a head. Then the spout became an arm and the handle another arm. Finally two legs sprouted out of the base. It sprang off the hibachi and danced wildly round the room. It ran up the walls, bounding about like a kitten, until the old man was

terrified that his beautiful room would be spoilt. He chased the kettle round and round until finally he managed to push it into a wooden box and shut the lid. While it rattled about in the box, he sat down panting, and tried to think what he should do with this troublesome creature. "It must be bewitched," he said to himself.

Just then, a junkman named Jimmu knocked at the door and asked if the old man had anything to sell. "What luck," thought the old man, "I can sell him the box with the kettle inside."

He lifted the lid of the box a little way to see if the kettle was quiet and to his amazement the head, legs and arms had vanished. It was an ordinary kettle again. It was very odd but the old man remembered how the fire had transformed it and decided that he still did not wish to keep it. So after a little bargaining over the price, Jimmu went on his way carrying the kettle.

Before Jimmu had gone very far he felt the kettle become heavier and heavier. By the time he got home that night, he was so tired he dumped the kettle down in a corner and fell asleep. Suddenly he was woken by a loud tapping sound. He looked round the room, but all he could see was the kettle lying quietly enough. He thought he must have been dreaming and fell asleep again, until he was woken a second time by even louder tap-tapping. He ran over to the corner, this time carrying a lamp, and saw to his astonishment that the kettle had grown a head, arms and legs, and was dancing! Then the kettle cartwheeled round the room out of sheer high spirits, turned a somersault and landed at Jimmu's feet.

"What – what are you?" stammered Jimmu.

"I am a magic tea-kettle," it answered. "Don't use me to make tea, as the old man you bought me from did. I hate to be filled with water and put on a hot hibachi. It is most painful. But I can be useful to you. I can dance, do acrobatics and walk the tightrope. Why don't you build a booth and we could put on a travelling show together? You would become rich that way."

Jimmu was delighted with this idea. The next day he built a booth and set out on his travels with the kettle.

Whenever Jimmu arrived at a village he would set up the booth and hang a notice on it asking people to come and witness the most amazing transformation ever seen. Everyone crowded round, and the kettle, looking quite ordinary, was passed from hand to hand. People were allowed to examine it and even to look inside. Then Jimmu took it back, placed it on the stage and commanded, "Dance, kettle, dance."

Instantly the lid began to turn into a head, the spout and the handle into arms, while two legs sprouted out of the base. Then the kettle gracefully performed the shadow dance and glided without pause into the fan dance and then the umbrella dance. It followed this with cartwheels and somersaults. At the climax of the show the kettle ran up on to a tightrope and waltzed across. The crowd always cried out with delight and showered the stage with coins.

As time went on, Jimmu and the kettle became very rich. They thought they had worked long enough and that it was time to retire and enjoy themselves. But Jimmu was an honest man and felt he owed some of his money to the old man who had sold him the kettle. So one fine morning he picked up the kettle and walked to the pretty little house in the high hills. He explained how the kettle had made his fortune and gave the old man a hundred gold pieces. The old man thanked him and said that few men would be as honest as Jimmu. Together they placed the tea-kettle in the Morinji temple in the city of Tatebayashi, where it was treated with great honor. It is said to be still among the treasures there to this day.

The Pumpkins of Witch Crunch

MARGARET MAHY

Three old men once lived side by side in a small town. Mr Hawthorne lived on the right, Mr Lavender on the left, and Mr Maverick-Mace between them. "A rose between two thorns," he used to say, though everyone else thought it was a thorn between two roses, for Mr Maverick-Mace was a very prickly man.

These three were very keen gardeners, but their gardens were quite different. Mr Hawthorne's garden sprawled and mingled, the cabbages wandering among the daffodils. Mr Lavender's garden was much neater, but a large tree grew on his lawn.

"You should cut that tree down," Mr Maverick-Mace told him. "The roots are ruining my garden, too."

"Oh well, the birds love it," said Mr Lavender, "and so do I." He put a bird-bath under the tree and planted crocuses around its knobby roots.

Mr Maverick-Mace's garden was like an army drilling. The plants went in straight lines, and the ground around them was bare and brown. He mostly grew vegetables to sell, but he also had a few flowers to enter in flower shows. They were bigger

and brighter than any flowers Mr Hawthorne or Mr Lavender grew. But if he saw anyone looking over his hedge to admire them, Mr Maverick-Mace felt sure they were planning to steal them. He frowned and became very rude until whoever it was hurried on. Then he'd walk off to shout soldierly orders to his terrified and cowering beets.

Now, up the road from the three gardeners lived Mrs Mehetibel, a little woman who wore skirts bright with patches. "My skirts are *my* garden," she would say. "Every time I sew on a patch, it's like planting a new flower."

Needless to say, Mr Maverick-Mace did not speak to this woman. He suspected she might be after his prize flowers.

One spring the word got out that pumpkins were going to be in short supply, and Mr Maverick-Mace immediately decided to plant some. He disliked their straggly gypsy ways, but he thought it was worth putting up with pumpkins if they were going to be scarce. They might make his fortune.

As he was bent over his garden, a voice came across the front fence. To his horror he saw it was Mrs Mehetibel.

"You've got a fine garden there," she called out. "And your cabbages are lovely. Could you spare one for a poor woman?"

Mr Maverick-Mace stood up furiously. "No, Madam, I couldn't," he declared. "It would spoil the appearance of the row. I grow cabbages to sell, not to give to any old witch."

There was silence for a moment, then the woman replied, "Witch you have said, witch it shall be." And she went on up the road. Mr Maverick-Mace suddenly felt alarmed. "That *was* Mrs Mehetibel, wasn't it . . .? That patched figure with the red scarf tied around her head. The voice was certainly hers—or was it?" he wondered.

Mr Lavender looked over the hedge. "You're a brave man," he said, "to speak to Mrs Mehetibel's sister like that!"

"Sister?" repeated Mr Maverick-Mace.

"Her twin sister—the well-known witch Ginger Crunch," Mr Lavender declared. "I try to be polite to everyone, but I'd be *extra* polite to Witch Crunch!"

"I don't believe in witches," said Mr Maverick-Mace in a sulky voice.

But when he came to plant the pumpkin seeds, he found they had turned blue. This worried him for a moment, but then he laughed. "Why, if the pumpkins grow blue, it will make my fortune all the same. People may not want to eat them, but they'll pay to look at them!"

He could hardly wait for the pumpkins to start growing—but when they did, they were just ordinary pumpkins. Mr Maverick-Mace was quite disappointed, and he was so nasty to his garden that two rows of red radishes turned white.

At first the pumpkins grew quietly. They were fine and green, and Mr Maverick-Mace grinned with delight, thinking of the hundreds of pumpkins he would sell.

They grew and grew. They put out green arms and a thousand twining fingers. They went up over Mr Hawthorne's fence and terrified his sweet peas. Mr Maverick-Mace's onions grew nervous and shuffled out of line, spoiling the look of the garden. Now Mr Maverick-Mace was not quite so happy. "You pumpkins!" he grumbled. Then he cheered up a bit. "Never mind! It's good to see you growing so well."

"They're growing *too* quickly for me," Mr Hawthorne said over the fence. "It isn't natural. You can practically *see* them move over the ground." He slapped away a wandering tendril of pumpkin that seemed to be trying to snatch off his glasses. "Those aren't pumpkins—those are pets, and not very well-trained ones! You need to put them on a collar and chain."

"Jealous!" thought Mr Maverick-Mace. But the next morning he was not at all pleased. The pumpkins had spread themselves over the onions and were busy pulling out the carrots. Mr Maverick-Mace was furious. "You pestilential pumpkins!" he shouted. "I'll rip you! I'll clip you!" He ran for the garden shears, but when he returned the pumpkins started to rustle and hiss. Their arms reared up like angry blind serpents.

Suddenly Mr Maverick-Mace was terrified. "I really

wouldn't dream of clipping you," he whined. "I just want to prune the hedge a little." He attacked the innocent hedge, but he could feel the pumpkins watching him and whispering to each other. Mr Maverick-Mace did not quite dare to turn his back on the pumpkins, but he did not want to watch them either. At last he scuttled inside.

The next few days were the worst Mr Maverick-Mace had ever spent. His garden was not his own any more—it belonged to the fiendish pumpkins! They pulled out his carrots and played marbles with his radishes. Every now and then Mr Maverick-Mace would go rushing out with an axe to cut back the rebellious pumpkin plants. But they always hissed at him furiously, lifting up their snaky arms to threaten him. Mr Maverick-Mace was too scared to threaten back.

Then one night as he sat trying to read his old gardening magazines, something happened—a tapping at his windows, the scratching of a thousand green fingers.

"Go away," whispered Mr Maverick-Mace. "Go away." But the pumpkins knocked more and more loudly. Then with a crash the door burst open, the windows broke, and the pumpkins rushed in at him.

"Help! Help!" he yelled. "The pumpkins are after me —*help!*"

In the cottage on the right Mr Hawthorne woke. In the house on the left Mr Lavender put down his paper. Then together they rushed out to rescue Mr Maverick-Mace. Mr Hawthorne carried his great-grandfather's sword, and Mr Lavender rode his lawn mower. Both attacked the pumpkins, which were now hissing like an angry sea. At first they took the pumpkins by surprise. The mower slashed into them, and Mr Hawthorne's waving sword whipped off several long snaky arms. But the pumpkins soon realized what was happening and choked the mower with their bristly leaves. They dragged Mr Lavender off and wrapped themselves around him. Mr Hawthorne's sword was twitched from his hand, and a strong pumpkin arm twisted itself around his ankles and tripped him. It was obvious the pumpkins were winning easily. Mr Lavender and Mr Hawthorne had almost given up when suddenly they saw Witch Crunch watching them with some amusement.

"It's a fine night for a bit of excitement," she observed, "and the moonlight looks lovely on the pumpkins, doesn't it?"

Mr Hawthorne and Mr Lavender were too choked by pumpkins to reply.

"Ah well," Ginger Crunch went on, "I've no wish to harm you, so I'd better whistle my pets to follow me to my burrow in the hills."

As she spoke, she took from her belt a long slender pipe and began to play a tune. The pumpkins stopped fighting and listened. Then, leaving the two men lying bruised and breathless, that army of terrible pumpkins pulled up their own roots and, like rippling serpents, gentle and docile, followed the witch and her strange piping tune. Down the hill she led them, and Mr Hawthorne and Mr Lavender watched her disappear with her strange pumpkins following and frolicking around her. As they stared, Mr Maverick-Mace stumbled out of the house. His clothes were in rags, his hair was standing on end, and he had a black eye that he had given himself in his struggle with the pumpkins. But, bruises and all, he was alive and safe and so glad to see the last of the pumpkins that he wept and promised to lead a new life full of kindness.

But, alas, it takes more than mad pumpkins to change a man

like Mr Maverick-Mace. As soon as his black eye was better, he became as crotchety as ever. However, he was very careful to be polite to Mrs Mehetibel and to send her bundles of vegetables. He was worried that she might otherwise write to the fiendish Ginger Crunch, and that one moonlit night those pumpkins might come writhing back up the hill to finish their work.

The Table and the Chair

EDWARD LEAR

Said the Table to the Chair,
'You can hardly be aware,
'How I suffer from the heat,
'And from chilblains on my feet!
'If we took a little walk,
'We might have a little talk!
'Pray let us take the air!'
Said the Table to the Chair.

Said the Chair unto the Table,
'Now you *know* we are not able!
'How foolishly you talk,
'When you know we *cannot* walk!'
Said the Table, with a sigh,
'It can do no harm to try,
'I've as many legs as you,
'Why can't we walk on two?'

55

So they both went slowly down,
And walked about the town
With a cheerful bumpy sound,
As they toddled round and round.
And everybody cried,
As they hastened to their side,
'See! The Table and the Chair
'Have come out to take the air!'

But in going down an alley,
To a castle in a valley,
They completely lost their way,
And wandered all the day,
Till, to see them safely back,
They paid a Ducky-quack,
And a Beetle, and a Mouse,
Who took them to their house.

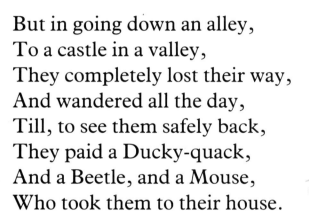

Then they whispered to each other,
'O delightful little brother!
'What a lovely walk we've taken!
'Let us dine on Beans and Bacon!'
So the Ducky, and the leetle
Browny-Mousy and the Beetle
Dined, and danced upon their heads
Till they toddled to their beds.

The Lonely Skyscraper
JENNY HAWKESWORTH

There was once a very tall skyscraper who stood by himself in the middle of many roads. The roads went over and under each other and round and round. Sometimes they disappeared into the ground and came up again a long way off. All the skyscraper could see was roads, stretching into the distance. During the day, cars and buses whizzed by and lorries thundered past in all directions.

The skyscraper was full of people who worked in him. They banged his doors and talked and laughed. They zoomed up and down in his lifts and swished in and out of his automatic doors.

Some of the people scrubbed and polished him until he gleamed more than ever before. But he was sad, because he was nobody's home. At night, the skyscraper stood alone, feeling big and echoey inside. It got cold and dark and silent and he was very, very lonely.

One clear day in early spring, the skyscraper was looking at his view when, from his very top windows, he saw something green beyond the endless grey of the winding roads.

"I wonder what that is," he thought to himself. He had never seen the countryside, so he didn't know what it looked like. But every day after that, he gazed into the distance at the thin line of green. He could see houses far away, small and neat enough to fit under the trees. It all looked so peaceful.

"If only I could live there," sighed the skyscraper.

That night he made up his mind to go.

First he rocked to one side. All the pencils and typewriters flew across the room and crashed against the walls.

"OUCH!" he said.

Then he rocked to the other side. All the typewriters and pencils flew back across to the opposite walls.

"OUCH!" he said again.

Next, he took his first step. CRUNCH! The noise of the skyscraper walking was louder than the noise of all the cars and lorries put together.

By sunrise, he had walked across all the grey roads and had just reached the beginning of the countryside that he was

longing to see. For the first time in his life, the skyscraper heard birds singing. He smelled the fresh, spring flowers as they opened towards the sun. He passed trees with more green leaves on them than he could count. The muddy country path felt cool and comfortable after walking on the hard city streets.

As the sun rose, so did the skyscraper's spirits. BOOM! CRASH! TINKLE! he went, as he walked along. The sun's beams glinted and flashed on his many windows. He had changed from grey to pink and orange, with gleams of green where grass and trees shone in his glass. If he'd known how to whistle he certainly would have done, from sheer happiness.

Soon he came to a field with a stream running round it and some sleepy black and white cows munching on the thick grass.

"What a lovely place to live!" thought the skyscraper, and he walked right through the fence into the middle of the field.

"Help!" cried the cows. "A monster!" and they all ran away.

A few minutes later an angry farmer with a red face came running down the road, waving a large stick.

"Get off my land!" he shouted, and he beat his stick against the skyscraper's gleaming front doors. Of course, the sky-scraper hardly noticed the stick, although it was heavy. But he didn't like feeling unwanted, so he moved away slowly.

"Where can I go?" he wondered. "I'm too big to live here." He felt huge and ugly in the pretty green field.

Suddenly a voice said, "Don't tread on me!"

The skyscraper bent down his top floors and gazed at the ground. He saw a tiny brown bird.

"I'll show you a place to live," said the bird. "It's the most beautiful place in the world. Let me come in and I'll take you there." SWOOSH! The skyscraper opened his shiny doors and the little bird hopped in.

As spring turned into summer, they travelled on. When it rained, the skyscraper went BOOM! SPLASH! TINKLE! SPLOSH! through all the muddy puddles.

At last they came to a great forest.

"Here we are!" cried the little bird.

"How shall I get through all those trees?" asked the sky-scraper. But the trees bent aside to let him pass and he went BOOM! TINKLE! CRUNCH! SWISH! over the grassy floor.

They came to a space in the middle of the forest.

"This will do," said the little bird, so the skyscraper sat down. KERUMP! BOOM! BUMP!

Then he arranged himself comfortably on the moss and looked round in all directions to see what was near him.

From his front windows, he saw rolling hills and fields with sheep and cattle grazing quietly in the afternoon sun.

From one side, he saw the sea, with a steamer trailing smoke along the horizon, and fishing boats and seagulls.

From the other side, he saw a village with leafy lanes winding between small cottages and gardens full of pretty flowers.

Far behind him, he saw the grey line of the distant city.

"So much to see and hear and smell," thought the skyscraper.

When summer was over, birds arrived to nest in his trays. Squirrels stored nuts in his paper cups. Mice lived in drawers and cabinets. Pencils were nibbled up for nests. Badgers slept on sofas, and moles tunnelled under the thick carpets. At bedtime, rabbits wrapped their babies in typewriter ribbons. Small insects were bathed in the inkwells. Baby voles cut their teeth on files marked "IMPORTANT" and little mice were tucked into all sorts of beds.

The skyscraper soon got used to all the furry tickles and bumps, but one winter day there seemed to be more activity than usual.

"What is happening now?" he asked the little brown bird.

"We're getting ready for a party," she replied. "A skyscraper-warming party!"

"But I'm warm enough already," said the skyscraper, who did not feel the cold with all the animals inside him. But the bird had already flown off to find her friends.

In the main dining room, all the animals were busy laying out a tempting feast on the shiny table tops. Before long, the skyscraper began to glow in the dazzling light of the setting sun. It was time for the party to begin.

Soon, sounds of merry-making rang through the snowy forest and the skyscraper was amazed to find himself growing warmer and warmer. It was a special sort of warmth, which spread from his top floors right down to his basement. Even his draughty halls felt snug, and his windy staircase cosy.

He remembered when he had stood by himself at night feeling cold, sad and lonely. Suddenly he laughed out loud! Now he knew what a 'skyscraper-warming' party really meant.

At last he was somebody's HOME.

Riddles

Little Nancy Etticoat
In a white petticoat
And a red rose.
The longer she stands,
The shorter she grows.

In Spring I look gay
Deck'd in comely array,
In Summer more clothing I wear;
When colder it grows
I fling off my clothes,
And in Winter quite naked appear.

The Strange Teeth

NANCY BIRCKHEAD

Forty teeth have I complete,
Yet I've never learned to eat;
Sometimes black and sometimes white,
Yet I cannot even bite!

Answers: A CANDLE. A TREE. A COMB.

The Voracious Vacuum Cleaner

LAURA CECIL

There was an old woman who lived all alone in a bungalow. At times she wanted company and wondered if she should buy a cat or a dog. But she was a finicky old person who liked to keep her home spotlessly clean and she thought an animal would make it dirty.

One day the doorbell rang and there was a man standing on her doorstep holding a bulky parcel.

"Madam, allow me to show you our latest vacuum cleaner," he said. "It is called The Voracious. It will go anywhere, consume anything. There is no need to plug it in, so it can keep you company while you do the chores together. It is much more useful than a pet as it cleans up instead of messing everything. It doesn't need food either, just dust and rubbish."

When he unpacked The Voracious, the old woman saw that it did indeed look rather like an unusual pet. It had a sleek grey body and a long hose coming out of one end that looked like a neck. The broad nozzle on the end of the hose was like a head with a wide grinning mouth. When the man switched it on, it gave a low purr that sounded like, "I'm hunngree." The old woman was delighted. "It even talks!" she said, "I'll buy it."

When the man had gone, she eagerly began to try out The Voracious. Soon there was not a speck of dust left in the bungalow, but The Voracious still purred: "I'm hunngree, I'm hunngree."

"You are a greedy one," said the old woman affectionately. But as she turned round to find some more dust for it, there was a sound like "SCHRULLP SCHRULLP," and a rug whizzed into The Voracious Vacuum Cleaner's nozzle, quickly followed by some cushions, a small table and the television.

"Stop! Stop!" cried the old woman but The Voracious just said: "I'm hunngree, I'm hunngree."

This time it sounded more like a snarl than a purr. Next the sofa and two armchairs disappeared down it with an even louder SCHRULLP. As the furniture went down, the hose bulged like a python swallowing a goat.

68

"Stop it at once!" shrieked the old woman, but as she stretched out to switch off The Voracious, SCHRULLP SCHRULLP, down she went too and landed with a bump on the sofa inside.

After all this eating, The Voracious had grown to about the size of a van, but it still went on gobbling everything it could see. When it had swallowed everything in the bungalow, it rolled its way out into the street. There it met the milkman on his delivery round. He was carrying two crates of milk bottles. The Voracious was now the size of a truck and blocked the road.

The milkman said, "Please would you move out of my way."

"I'm Hunngree Hunngree Hunngree!" growled The Voracious Vacuum Cleaner and SCHRULLP SCHRULLP SCHRULLP down went the milkman, milk crates and all.

"Pity you don't have any tea with you," said the old woman, when the milkman and his bottles landed with a crash inside. "I could do with a cup right now."

By now The Voracious was the size of a bus. Round the corner came a class of school children with their teacher. They had been to the library and each clutched a book.

"Let the children pass," cried the teacher.

"I'm HUNNGREE HUNNGREE HUNNGREE!"

SCHRULLP SCHRULLP down went all the children and the teacher.

"Make yourselves comfortable and have some milk," said the old woman and the milkman when the teacher and the children landed in a heap on the sofa.

Now The Voracious was as large as a cottage and it rolled into

the High Street. Just then a crowd of young men going to a football match came face to face with it. They were dressed in bright hats and scarves and they were singing their team song. Before they could pause for breath The Voracious roared:

"I'm HUNNGREE HUNNGREE HUNNGREE!"

And SCHRULLP SCHRULLP SCHRULLP SCHRULLP down the hose they all went still singing, "Here we go! Here we go! Here we go!"

"You can make yourselves useful and read to the children," said the old woman, the milkman and the teacher when the football fans tumbled on to the sofa.

Next a great yellow crane came rumbling up the road. With it was a team of builders in yellow overalls and hard hats. They were on their way to a building site. The Voracious was now the size of a house. "Move yourself, mate!" shouted the crane driver.

"I'm HUNNGREE HUNNGREE HUNNGREE!" The Voracious bellowed, and SCHRULLP SCHRULLP SCHRULLP SCHRULLP down went the crane and the builders.

"Oh, we are glad to see you," said the old woman, the milkman, the teacher, the children and the football fans when the crane and the builders squeezed in. "Perhaps you'll be able to get us out of this monstrous machine." But the crane driver and the builders had no better ideas than anyone else.

Meanwhile The Voracious had grown to the size of a church, so it barely noticed a roller-skate lying lost in the road, though it swallowed it up all the same because the skate was in its path. But the skate had no intention of being swallowed right down inside The Voracious. Instead, it rolled into the vacuum cleaner's machinery before it could be swept on to the sofa like everyone else.

At that moment a big fire engine came screeching up the road, its sirens blaring. When the fire chief shouted "Out of our way!" The Voracious swelled even larger and reached out its nozzle, but the only sound that came out was CLICKHISS CLICKHISS CLICKHISS CLUNK CLUNK. The roller-skate had jammed the works. The body of The Voracious went on swelling as it tried to swallow until there was a loud BOOM!

There, sitting among the wreckage, were the old lady, the milkman, the teacher, the children, the football fans, the builders and their crane. They were all extremely dusty and very happy to be out.

Everyone helped the old woman take her furniture back into her bungalow. She saw the roller-skate glinting in the rubble and, thinking that it might come in useful, took it back as well.

It proved very useful indeed because after that the old woman did not like to use a vacuum cleaner. Instead, she scooted round the bungalow on the skate whenever she did her sweeping. This made it a much quicker job. And she was never lonely again because she had made so many friends inside The Voracious Vacuum Cleaner.

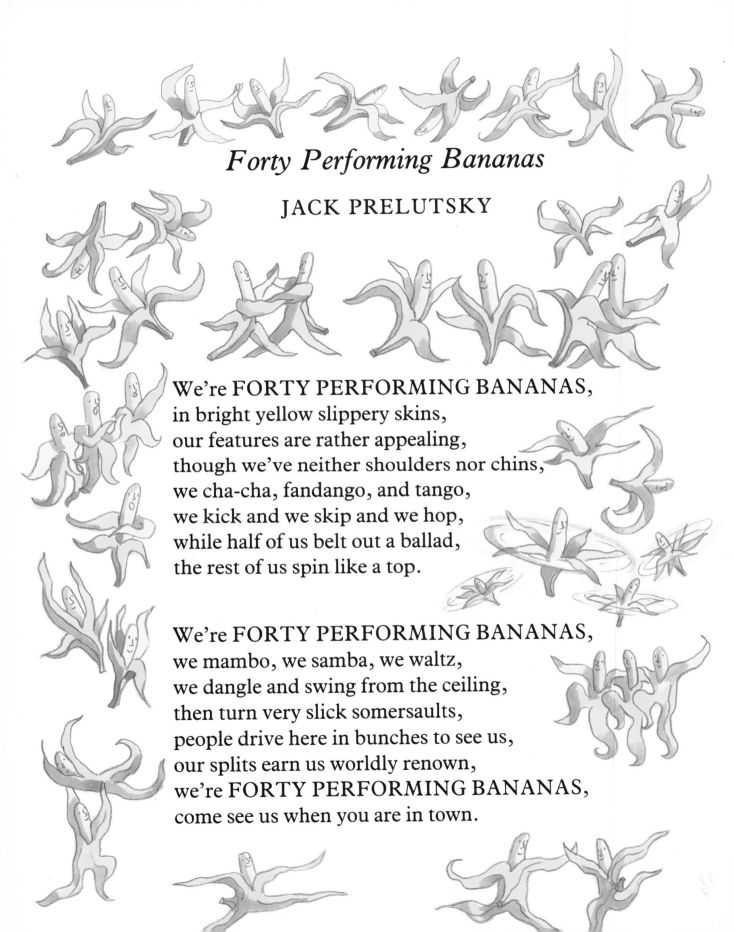

Forty Performing Bananas

JACK PRELUTSKY

We're FORTY PERFORMING BANANAS,
in bright yellow slippery skins,
our features are rather appealing,
though we've neither shoulders nor chins,
we cha-cha, fandango, and tango,
we kick and we skip and we hop,
while half of us belt out a ballad,
the rest of us spin like a top.

We're FORTY PERFORMING BANANAS,
we mambo, we samba, we waltz,
we dangle and swing from the ceiling,
then turn very slick somersaults,
people drive here in bunches to see us,
our splits earn us worldly renown,
we're FORTY PERFORMING BANANAS,
come see us when you are in town.

Brown Paper
ALISON UTTLEY

Once there lived a sheet of brown paper, which lay on a shelf in a small newspaper shop. It lay flat, dry, dull, and it felt thirsty and eager to be off on adventures. It could not move a fiber, it was folded so tightly, and it could scarcely breathe.

After some months, which it spent in sleep, the papers over it were sold, and at last the brown paper was bought, for it was Christmas time and many parcels had to be wrapped. It was picked up, and carried away and taken to a house where the children ran to help to unpack the basket.

"This is a lovely clean sheet of paper," they cried as they took it out and spread it on the table. "We must use this for something special."

It was unfolded, the creases were smoothed, and then it lay on the white table while a parcel was packed to go inside it. The box had a red ribbon around it, and the brown paper stared in astonishment. It hoped it also would have a red ribbon, but the box was placed on it, and the paper neatly folded and bent at the edges so that it held the ribboned box firmly within its embrace. A length of string was fixed around and tied with many knots, but there was no ribbon outside.

"Nobody can untie these knots," said one of the children and the paper echoed: "Nobody can untie my knots."

"Did you hear it squeak?" asked another child. "It talked, I heard it. What did it say?"

"It said: 'I'm going off by post to bring a present to my grandmother'," said the smiling mother, patting the parcel as if it were a little brown dog.

She lighted a candle, and held a stick of sealing-wax in the flame. The parcel was alarmed when the hot wax touched it, for it thought it was going to be set on fire. Then it smiled as the wax cooled into little red knobs like flowers and beads. Each little knob was sealed with a dragon seal, and it looked very fine.

"Goodbye, parcel," cried the children. "Goodbye," answered the parcel, and the mother took it to the post office with many another parcel.

"I'm going on an adventure," boasted the parcel, and the brown paper was tossed here and there, but it was so stout and strong it never tore in spite of the rough treatment it received. It was stamped, and thrown into a basket, and taken by train and packed in a hamper, and carried in a bag.

There was not time to talk to the other parcels, and the brown paper was glad it had the scarlet knobs like dragons to hold the string, and the warm red ribbon cheered it and kept its heart happy.

It was taken by the postman to the grandmother's house, and the old lady untied the knots with great care, and removed the knobs of wax. She folded the string and put it away. Then she removed the brown paper, and took out the box with the red ribbons.

"At last!" sighed the paper, crackling its sides. "Now I shall see what is inside that box."

She took out a pair of bedroom slippers, dark red with white fur linings and white fur bows on the top.

"Oh, how lovely," cried the grandmother, and at once she slipped them on her feet and walked up and down admiring them. She folded the ribbon and put it away in a drawer with her handkerchiefs, but the paper too she folded and stroked and put in a drawer where more paper lay.

It was a nice wide drawer in the kitchen dresser, and through the crack the paper could see the old lady's pots and pans, the bright fire and the shining saucepans and the cat on the stool. A clock ticked the hours away and chimed like a bell. A musical box played a tune, and the cat purred.

"I am happy," sang the brown paper and the kettle sang too.

Brown paper, brown paper,
what do you see?
'A kitchen, a fire,
And a brown cup of tea.'
Brown paper, brown paper,
What do you think?
'I love the brass saucepan
on bright kitchen sink.'
Brown paper, brown paper,
What will you do?
'I shall live in this drawer
for a month
or two.'

And the brown paper did live there for nearly three months, but when Easter came it was taken out, and smoothed, and then folded round the same box tied with a red ribbon. The old lady crossed out her own address and put the address of the house where her grandchildren lived. The brown paper did not know this, for it couldn't read, but it was pleased to be wrapping itself about the same cardboard box.

The string was tied in many knots and sealed with scarlet wax once more. "Goodbye, kitchen, goodbye," called the brown paper. Then it was taken to the post office and its journey began again. It was thrown about, it was tossed on to a heap of parcels, it was examined now and then.

"With Care" was written in large letters, and everyone smiled at "With Care" for nobody took any care at all. Only the paper gripped the cardboard box tightly to prevent any damage, and the cardboard box held its shoulders firmly and refused to be broken or squashed.

At last, after many troubles, the parcel was put in a sack and taken to the home of the children.

When the postman tapped at the door and held out the parcel, the brown paper gave a quiver of joy and it began to whisper in its little soft voice.

"Here I am, home again. There's the village street where I lay on the shelf of the newspaper shop and here's the lady who bought me. Here are the children, all smiling at me, and here's the little dog."

"Don't open until Easter Sunday," said the mother and she put the parcel on the spare-room bed. On Easter Sunday it was taken downstairs to the breakfast table, and it lay on the white cloth, among the cups and saucers.

"A parcel from Grannie," cried the children. "Easter eggs, I expect."

The mother untied the string, and removed the crumpled paper. She untied the red ribbon and opened the cardboard box, and she took out four small Easter eggs. Two were made of chocolate, one was made of blue velvet, and the fourth was made of wood.

Inside the wooden egg was a yellow chicken, but inside the blue velvet egg was a silver thimble.

"Oh, what lovely presents," cried the children. "The blue egg is yours, Mother, it says so, and the wooden egg is Daddy's, and the two chocolate eggs are ours."

"It's the same paper we had at Christmas," said one of the children, examining the brown paper and finding their mother's writing on it. "Just fancy. It has come home again. I wonder if it is glad!"

"Of course it isn't. Paper can't feel," said the little boy's elder sister, so the paper crackled its sides and whispered loudly: "I *am* glad. I *am* glad."

"It *is* glad. It says so," said the little boy. "Please can I have it for my own piece of paper?"

"Yes, darling, if you really want it," said his mother. So the little boy, whose name was Paul, took the paper to his bedroom.

One of his Easter presents was a paint box. He decided to make a picture on the brown paper. So he fetched some water, and began to paint. He made a tree on one side, with great branches curling over the paper, and in the boughs he placed a bird. What was it? He thought it was a wood pigeon, for it was pale grey and it had a ring of white round its neck.

Then he painted the roots of the tree, going down under the green grass, right down to the warm brown soil, and among the roots he made little houses, one for field mice, another for a

mole, and another for a grass snake. He painted flowers, flowers growing in the grass, primroses and violets and daisies. He made a rabbit hole, with Mrs Rabbit living down in her house, and lots of baby rabbits sitting on the grass near.

Then he painted the sky, pale blue with a white cloud, and an aeroplane flying across.

His mother peeped through the open door. "What are you doing, Paul?" she asked. "You are very quiet."

"I'm making a picture on my brown paper," said Paul, and he showed it to his mother.

"It's a fine picture, Paul. The best you have ever done. I do believe that pigeon is going to call," and sure enough a wood pigeon called "Coo-roo. Coo-roo."

The rabbits flicked their white tails, the grass snake moved down into its hole, the tree shook its branches.

Then all was still and quiet again.

"I really thought the picture was alive," said the mother. "It's all imagination, of course, but I thought I saw things move."

"They did move, Mother. It's because I painted on this brown paper. Will you hang it up for me?"

So the mother fastened a tack in the wall and hung the picture there, just like a real picture. The tree kept very still, the bird did not sing, the flowers were asleep, but when Paul went to bed that night he could hear a gentle "Coo-roo. Coo-roo," coming from the wood pigeon's throat, and he heard the rustle of the leaves, and the faraway sound of the plane.

Then he fell fast asleep, but the brown paper was very much alive.

"I am happy, happy, happy," it sang. "For now I am a real painting, hung on the wall, for all to see."

As I Passed By

ANON

As I passed by my little pigsty,
I saw a petticoat hanging to dry,
Hanging to dry, hanging to dry,
I saw a petticoat hanging to dry.

I took off my jacket and laid it hard by,
To bear the petticoat company,
Company, company,
To bear the petticoat company.

The wind blew high and down they fell,
Jacket and petticoat into the well,
Into the well, into the well,
Jacket and petticoat into the well.

85

"Oh, oh!" says the jacket, "we shall be drowned,"
"Oh, no!" says the petticoat, "we shall be found."
"Oh, yes!" says the jacket, "we shall be drowned,"
"Oh, no!" says the petticoat, "we shall be found."

The miller passed, they gave a shout,
He put in his hand and he pulled them both out,
Pulled them both out, pulled them both out,
He put in his hand and he pulled them both out.

Don't Blame Me!
RICHARD HUGHES

There was once a young man called Simon, who lived a long way from where he worked. So he thought, "If I could only buy a nice motor-bike to go to my work on, that would be fine." So Simon saved up his money, till he thought he had nearly enough; and one Saturday he went off to the street where second-hand motor-bikes were sold, to see if he could find one to suit him.

At almost the first shop he came to, there was a most grand-looking motor-bike, almost new; and the price the man was asking seemed much too cheap for such a fine one. So Simon said he would buy it; but all the man said was, "Don't blame me!"—which seemed to Simon a funny thing to say.

Simon bought it, and rode it home; and it went sweetly and well, and he was very pleased with it. So on Monday morning he started out on it to his work; and as he went he wondered what the man who sold it meant when he said, "Don't blame me!"

Simon knew soon enough, though; for as he was riding along a lonely piece of road, he felt the motor-bike beginning to wriggle under him, as if it was coming to bits. It wasn't doing that, but it was doing something far worse—it was turning into a crocodile!

When Simon found he was riding a crocodile, he was more frightened than he had ever been before. He was too frightened to stay on its back; so he jumped off, and began to run for his life with the crocodile after him; and at first he left the crocodile a bit behind.

But presently Simon began to get so tired that the crocodile began to catch him up, and he thought he would have to give up and be eaten. Just then he saw a donkey in the road before him. He managed to run till he had caught up the donkey, and then he said:

"Mr Donkey, will you kindly give me a ride?"

But the donkey was a selfish one, not a nice donkey at all; and just because he saw Simon was really tired and needed a ride, he said, No, he wouldn't.

"You can jolly well walk," he said. "*I* have to!"

"All right," said Simon; "then let me pass you," for the road was rather narrow.

So the donkey let him pass; and Simon walked. Now that he had the donkey in between him and the crocodile he didn't feel quite so frightened; so he didn't trouble to walk very fast.

Presently the donkey said:

"Hee-haw! Hee-haw! Simon, Simon, will you walk a little faster? There's a crocodile behind me, and he's snapped off my tail."

But Simon wouldn't trouble to walk faster, and the donkey couldn't pass him to get away from the crocodile; so presently the donkey said:

"Hee-haw! Hee-haw! HEE-HAW! *Will* you walk a little faster, *please*? There's a crocodile behind me, and he's swallowed me all but my head."

But even then Simon wouldn't trouble to walk any faster; and then at last he heard the donkey say in a faint, small voice:

"Hee-haw! Hee-haw! I'm *inside* the crocodile now!"

So then Simon knew he would have to run again, so away he

went for his life, with the crocodile after him. But because he had had a good rest, at first he left the crocodile behind; and also, of course, the crocodile had a heavy donkey inside him now.

Presently in the road ahead of him Simon saw a giant.

"Mr Giant," said Simon to the giant, "will you kindly give me a ride?"

"Certainly!" said the giant kindly. "Certainly, certainly, certainly!" So he picked up Simon and sat him on his shoulder, and went on strolling along the road, swinging his umbrella as he went.

Presently Simon saw the crocodile catching them up; but he didn't tell the giant, because he didn't quite know what to say.

"Ow!" the giant cried suddenly, and began to dance. "I've been stung by a wasp!"

When the giant danced it was difficult for Simon to hold on; but somehow he managed, and looking down he saw what had really happened. It wasn't a wasp, it was the crocodile who had bitten the giant, and who was holding on to the seat of the giant's trousers like grim death.

But the giant couldn't see that, because it was behind him and his neck was stiff. He just kept on dancing and swishing behind him with his umbrella. And though Simon was sorry to have got the kind giant into so much trouble, he wasn't going to let go. He just hung on and hoped for the best.

At last, by great good luck, the giant managed to hit the crocodile with his umbrella. Now, giants' umbrellas are generally magic, and this one certainly was. For no sooner did it touch the crocodile, than the crocodile turned back again into a motor-bike, and just then Simon lost hold of the giant's collar and fell in the road with a frightful thump on his head.

The thump knocked him silly at first, but presently he sat up and opened his eyes. There was the motor-bike lying in the road; a crowd of people was standing around.

"That's a nice motor-bike you've got," said one of them. "Do you want to sell it?"

"Yes," said Simon.

"Then I'll buy it," said the other chap.

"All right," said Simon, "buy it if you like, but *Don't Blame Me!*"

For Simon saw then what none of the others saw. He saw the motor-bike open its mouth and grin with all its wicked white teeth. And no wonder the motor-bike was pleased! For the young man who had bought it now was fat and juicy, and didn't look as if *he* could run an inch!